THE ADVENTURES OF FIREMAN
THE CASE OF THE STINGER

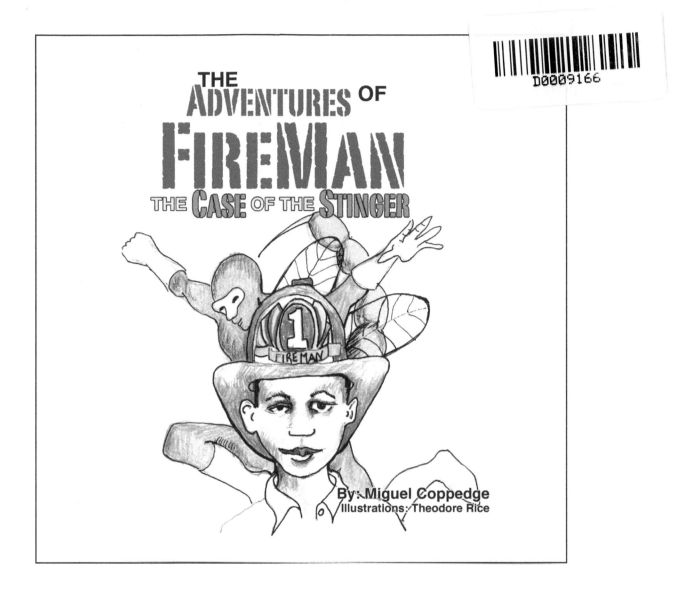

By: Miguel Coppedge
Illustrations: Theodore Rice

Halo ● ● ●
Publishing International

ISBN 13: 978-1-61244-487-1
Library of Congress Control Number: 2016946083

Printed in the United States of America

Halo
Publishing International
www.halopublishing.com

Published by Halo Publishing International
1100 NW Loop 410
Suite 700 - 176
San Antonio, Texas 78213
Toll Free 1-877-705-9647
www.halopublishing.com
www.holapublishing.com
e-mail: contact@halopublishing.com

I dedicate this book to my mommy Yolanda Coppedge, my daddy Magale Narce, my granddaddy Van Coppedge, my 3rd grade teacher Mrs. Robinson, my art teacher Mr. Theodore Rice for the Awesome illustrations, President Barack Obama, and my publisher Ms. Lisa Umina for continuing to believe in me and being the best publisher EVER! Last but not least my football team The Metropolitan Wolverines. If I didn't get stung by the bee at our football game, this book wouldn't exist. Thank you all for believing in me. I love you!

Miguel Coppedge
A.K.A.
FireMan

Foreword

In the last Adventures of FireMan, Kris Schmoove and Rico G. retired from being super heroes to focus on being regular teenagers. Will they come out of retirement? Sit back and relax and enjoy the next Adventure!

Kris and Rico were relaxing on the beach enjoying their retirement. "I'm so glad we don't have to fight crime Rico," said Kris. "Me too!" replied Rico.

While Kris and Rico were chilling in the sun, they all of a sudden see people running and screaming with humongous red bumps on their bodies.

Little did they know that their arch enemies The Destroyer and Bang were behind all the dismay. They used their pet bee the "The Stinger" to start ruckus.

The Stinger stung anyone who was in his way. He purposely missed Kris and Rico because he had another plan to strike and that's when he'll get them.

The next incident happened at a football game. Some kids were playing around outside of the field during the game. That's when The Stinger decided to attack. He started stinging everyone in sight!

Kris and Rico saw everything! That's when Kris said, "Rico it's time to come out of retirement and kick some Stinger Butt!" Up, Up and Away! It's time for us to save the day!

FireMan and The Time Slower started battling with The Stinger. All of a sudden FireMan got stung. But he didn't know he was allergic to bee stings until he swelled up.

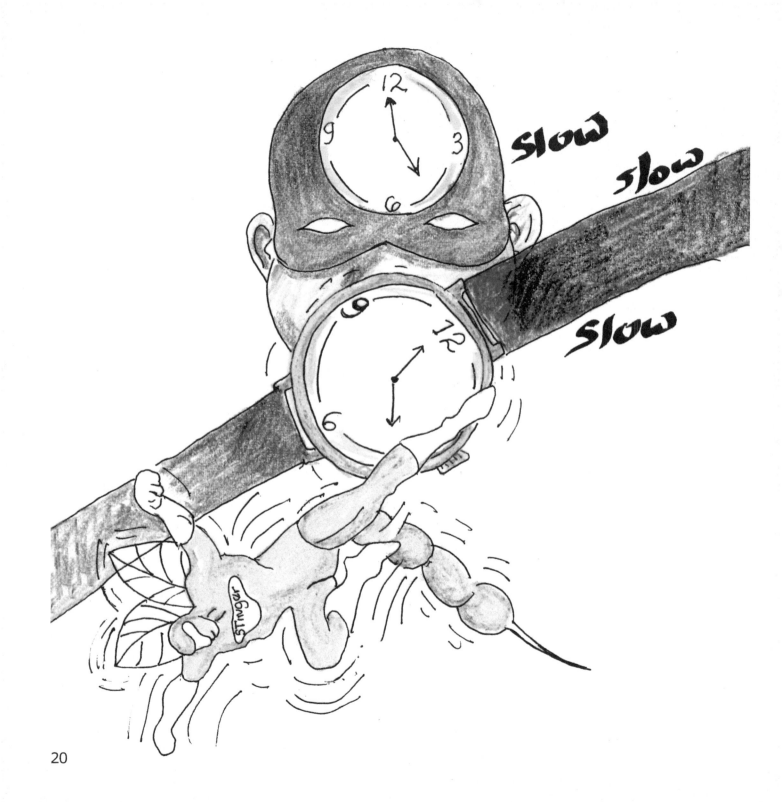

The Time Slower was left alone to defeat The Stinger. So he slowed down time to stop The Stinger so that he could help FireMan. He had to find a cure to stop him from swelling.

"Donuts! I need Donuts! Said Fireman in a faint voice. It will stop the swelling and give me strength to defeat The Stinger". You got it! The Time Slower found some donuts and fed them to FireMan. He was cured and got his powers back.

FireMan used his fire power to burn off The Stinger's stinger. "You won't be stinging anyone else anymore!" Said FireMan.

The Stinger was sent away to live in a hive facility for bad bees never to be seen again.

Once again FireMan and The Time Slower saved the day! It's a good thing they came out of retirement. Hip, Hip Hooray! The world is safe again!

CPSIA information can be obtained
at www.ICGtesting.com
Printed in the USA
BVOW05*1944230118
506090BV00004B/13/P